Little Red
Riding Hood

PaRrag

Bath · New York · Cologne · Melbourne · D
Hong Kong · Shenzhen · Singapore · Amste

D1444329

This book belongs to

....

This edition published by Parragon Books Ltd in 2015 and distributed by

Parragon Inc.
440 Park Avenue South, 13th Floor
New York, NY 10016
www.parragon.com

Copyright © Parragon Books Ltd 2012–2015

Illustrated by Dubravka Kolanovic
Reading consultant: Geraldine Taylor

ISBN 978-1-4748-0829-3

Printed in China

Little Red
Riding Hood

Five steps for enjoyable reading

Traditional stories and fairy tales are a great way to begin reading practice. The stories and characters are familiar and lively. Follow the steps below to help your child become a confident and independent reader:

Step 1
Read the story aloud to your child. Run your finger under the words as you read.

In a faraway wood lived a kind girl named Little Red Riding Hood. She was taking a basket of food to her sick grandma.

"Remember," said her mother, "go straight to Grandma's house, don't stray off the path, and don't talk to any strangers!"

8

Step 2
Look at the pictures and talk about what is happening.

Step 3

Read the simple text on the right-hand page together. When reading, some words come up again and again, such as **the**, **to**, **and**. Your child will quickly get to recognize these high-frequency words by sight.

Little Red Riding Hood set off to see her grandma.

9

Step 4

When your child is ready, encourage them to read the simple lines on their own.

Step 5

Help your child to complete the puzzles at the back of the book.

In a faraway wood lived a kind girl named Little Red Riding Hood. She was taking a basket of food to her sick grandma.

"Remember," said her mother, "go straight to Grandma's house, don't stray off the path, and don't talk to any strangers!"

Little Red Riding Hood set
off to see her grandma.

Little Red Riding Hood followed the path that wound through the woods. She hummed a little tune as she swung her basket of goodies. She saw lots of pretty blue flowers. But she didn't see the wolf hiding in the trees!

Little Red Riding
Hood stopped to look
at the blue flowers.

"Hello, little girl," said the Big Bad Wolf. "What are you doing?"

Little Red Riding Hood jumped with fright. "I'm going to see my sick grandma who lives in the little house in the woods," she said.

"What a kind girl you are," he smiled, showing his big, white teeth. "I'm sure your grandma will like these pretty blue flowers. Why don't you stay and pick some for her?"

The Big Bad Wolf ran off
into the woods.

While Little Red Riding Hood
stayed to pick some blue flowers,
the Big Bad Wolf ran all the
way to Grandma's house ...
and gobbled her up! He put on
Grandma's cap and glasses.

The Big Bad Wolf got
into Grandma's bed.

Soon after, Little Red Riding
Hood arrived at Grandma's
house. The door was wide open.
So Little Red Riding Hood
walked in.

"Are you in bed, Grandma?"
she called out.

Little Red Riding Hood went into
the bedroom. She walked up to the bed.
Grandma wasn't looking very well!

"Oh Grandma," she said, "what big
ears you have!"

"All the better to hear you with,
my dear," said the wolf in a
Grandma voice.

Grandma had very big ears!

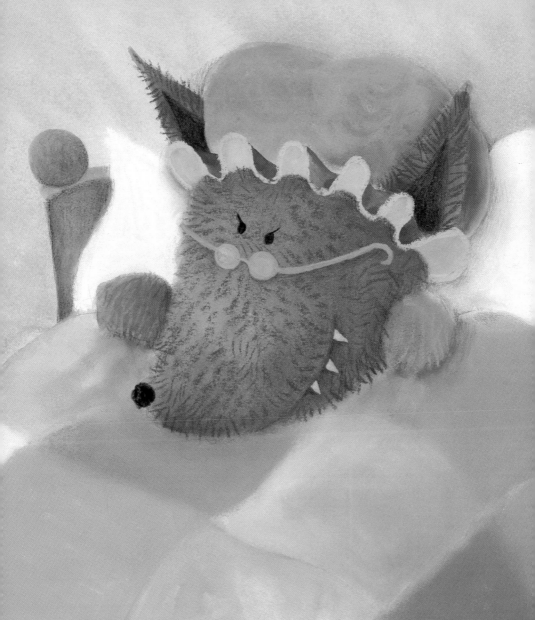

"Oh Grandma," said Little Red Riding Hood, "what big eyes you have!"

"All the better to see you with, my dear," said the wolf in his Grandma voice.

Little Red Riding Hood thought
Grandma looked strange.

"Oh Grandma," said Little Red Riding Hood, "what big teeth you have!"

"All the better to eat you with," growled the wolf. And he opened his mouth wide and leaped at Little Red Riding Hood.

The Big Bad Wolf ate Little Red
Riding Hood!

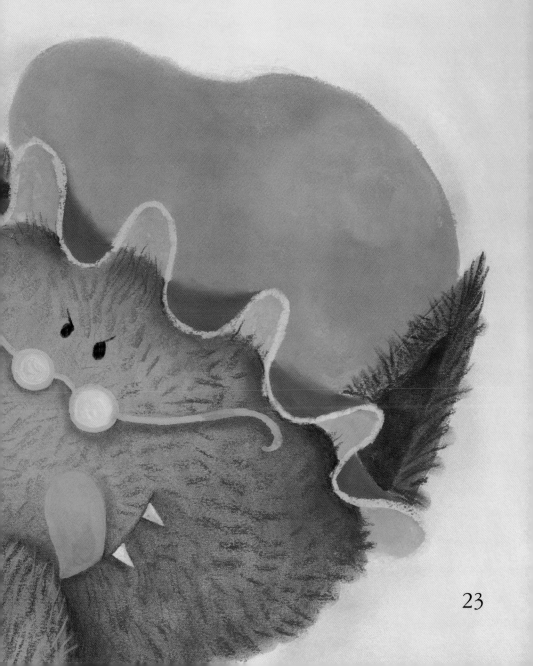

Luckily, a woodcutter was passing Grandma's cottage. He went in to visit Grandma and found the Big Bad Wolf taking a nap. He bashed the wolf with his ax. Then he turned the wolf upside down and gave him a good shake.

Out came Grandma and
Little Red Riding Hood!

Grandma, Little Red Riding
Hood, and the woodcutter waving
his ax all chased the Big Bad Wolf.
The Big Bad Wolf ran away.

And they never saw
him again.

Puzzle time!

Which two words rhyme?

see bed red bad big

Which word does not match
the picture?

ear

eyes

ax

Which word matches the picture?

good

wood

hood

Who has a basket?

Little Red Riding Hood

Grandma

woodcutter

Which sentence is right?

The Big Bad Wolf ran away.

The Big Bad Wolf ran back.